FOR LEAH

Copyright © 2017 by Dan Santat
Published by Roaring Brook Press
Roaring Brook Press is a division of
Holtzbrinck Publishing Holdings Limited Partnership
175 Fifth Avenue, New York, New York 10010
mackids.com
All rights reserved

Cataloging-in-Publication Data is on file at the Library of Congress

ISBN: 978-1-62672-682-6

Our books may be purchased in bulk for promotional, educational,
or business use. Please contact your local bookseller or the Macmillan
Corporate and Premium Sales Department at (800) 221-7945 ext. 5442
or by e-mail at MacmillanSpecialMarkets@macmillan.com.

First edition, 2017
Book design by Andrew Arnold
Printed in the United States of America by
Worzalla, Stevens Point, Wisconsin

7 9 10 8 6

AFTER the FALL

HOW HUMPTY DUMPTY GOT BACK UP AGAIN

a story by
DAN SANTAT

My name is Humpty Dumpty.

This was my favorite spot, high up on the wall.
I know, it's an odd place for an egg to be,
but I loved being close to the birds.

Then one day, I fell. (I'm sort of famous for that part.)

Folks called it "The Great Fall," which sounds a little grand.

It was just an accident.

But it changed my life.

KINGS COUNTY HOSPITAL

Fortunately, all the king's men managed to put me back together.

Well, most of me.

There were some parts that couldn't be healed with bandages and glue.

After that day, I became afraid of heights.

I was so scared that it kept me from enjoying some of my favorite things.

I walked past the wall every day, and I would think about climbing that ladder again.

I really missed the birds and being high above the city.

But I could never do it . . .

because I knew that accidents can happen.

I eventually settled for watching the birds from the ground.

It wasn't the same, but it was better than nothing.

Then one day, an idea flew by . . .

Making planes was harder than I thought.

It was easy to get cuts and scratches.

But, day after day, I kept trying . . .

. . . and trying . . .

until I got it just right.

My plane was perfect, and it flew like nothing could stop it.

I hadn't felt that happy in a long time.

It wasn't the same as being up in the sky with the birds,

but it was close enough.

Unfortunately, accidents happen . . .

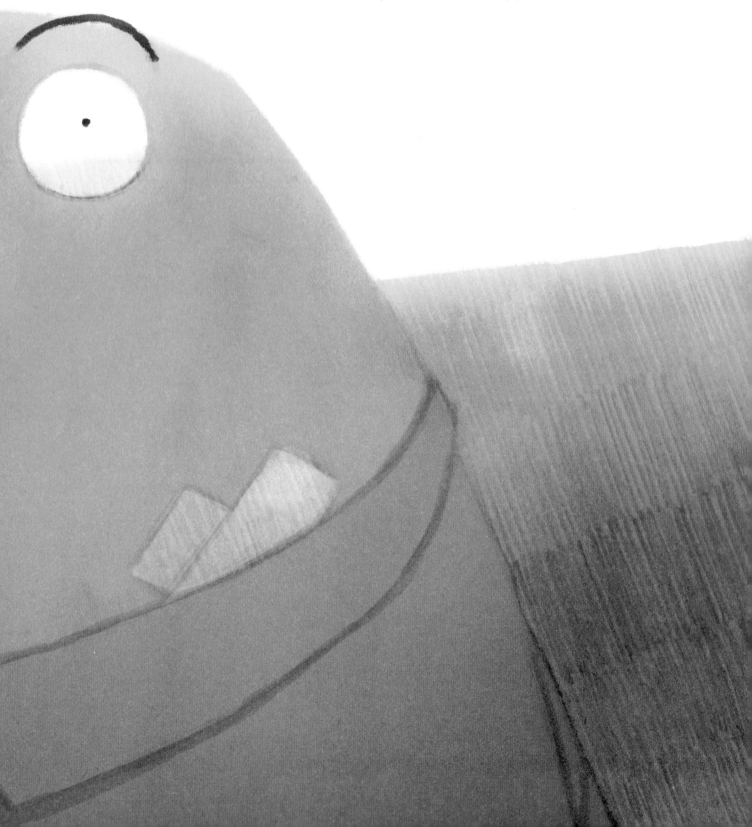

They always do.

I almost walked away, again.

But then I thought about all the time I'd spent working on my plane,
and all the other things I'd missed.

I decided I was going to climb that wall.

But the higher I got,

the more nervous I felt.

I didn't want to admit it:

I was terrified.

12

I didn't look up.

I didn't look down.

I just kept climbing.

One step at a time . . .

until I was no longer afraid.

Maybe now you won't think of me as that
egg who was famous for falling.

Hopefully, you'll remember me as the egg who got back up.

. . . and learned how to fly.